"𝒟awn, come for dinner," B's mom called. "Dawn! Oh, never mind. There's no stopping her practicing."

B swallowed a mouthful of dinner. It was bad enough having to demonstrate her magical skills to an audience and panel of judges. But living up to her older sister was impossible, plain and simple.

"Why the long face, B?" her dad asked.

"Oh, nothing," B said. "Pass the nachos, please."

DISCOVER ALL THE MAGIC!

B Magical

The Superstar Sister

By Lexi Connor

SCHOLASTIC INC.

New York   Toronto   London   Auckland
Sydney   Mexico City   New Delhi   Hong Kong

ISBN 978-0-545-11741-8

Copyright © 2010 by Working Partners Ltd.
Series created by Working Partners Ltd., London
All rights reserved. Published by Scholastic Inc.,
557 Broadway, New York, NY 10012.
SCHOLASTIC, APPLE PAPERBACKS, and associated logos are trademarks and/or registered trademarks of Scholastic Inc.

12 11 10 9 8 7 6 5 4 3 2 1   10 11 12 13 14 15/0

Printed in the U.S.A.   40
First printing, November 2010

Special thanks to Julie Berry

To Shirley

Chapter 1

Beatrix, or B for short, slid onto a kitchen stool and watched her mother work her magic. A brick of cheddar cheese shredded itself into a pile while an invisible knife diced a juicy red tomato. Her mother stood behind the counter, muttering spells under her breath.

"Tacos tonight, Mom?" B asked.

"Taco salad," Mrs. Cicely corrected. "Guacamole . . . let me think . . . Ah. Here we go.

Chips, sour cream, refried frijoles,
All we need is guacamole.
Mash garlic with avocado,
Onion, and a ripe to-mah-to."

And before B's eyes, two avocados peeled themselves in midair. They spat out their large round stones, plopped themselves in a bowl, and blended in with a swirl of garlic, onion, and tomato. Mrs. Cicely added a dash of salt, and B scooped up some of the finished guacamole with a tortilla chip. Delicious! Her mom definitely had a talent for cooking.

A loud drumbeat rattled through the kitchen ceiling, shaking the hanging lamps. B recognized the intro to "Swagger," a recent single from the Black Cats. They'd been her favorite band long before meeting her friend Trina, who turned out to be the lead singer. Trina had an amazing voice — and was also a witch, like B.

B pinched another chip and pointed it at the ceiling. "What's up?"

"It's your sister," Mrs. Cicely said. "She's been in her room ever since she got home from school, practicing her act for the talent show."

The whole city was buzzing with the news that the TV show *You've Got It!* was hosting auditions in B's school auditorium. The show was even bringing out its mega-famous host, Clifton Davro, to judge the auditions.

"Of course." B tried to snag more guacamole, but her mother whisked it away before she could reach the dish. "Everyone I know seems to be going crazy trying to find a winning act. George nearly choked on the bus trying to sing 'The Star-Spangled Banner' while eating Enchanted Chocolates."

Mrs. Cicely made a face. "That can't have been nice to watch."

B laughed at the memory of her best friend George's face smeared with chocolate, singing, "*Jo se can oo lee.*" At least that was what it had sounded like.

"Have *you* done any practicing for your performance?" her mom asked.

"Hah." It was B's turn to make a sour face. "My only talent is messing things up. I'm in no hurry to do that on national television. I'm pretty sure I don't *have it.*"

"I didn't mean the talent show," Mrs. Cicely said.

B could hear the edge of a lecture creeping into her mom's voice. "I was thinking of Friday's Young Witch Competition."

B's spirits drooped. All the excitement since the announcement from *You've Got It!* had almost made her forget about her opportunity for humiliation at the annual witching event. B hated being up onstage, and this competition would force her to compete in front of a huge crowd. While all the other witches would be making up original rhyming spells for the contest, B's magic was different. She cast spells by spelling words, and sometimes they had unexpected consequences. But the worst thing about the competition was that her sister had won it when she was eleven.

"I've been thinking about it a lot," B said, "but I haven't gotten far." She knew she needed something U-N-I-Q-U-E and A-W-E-S-O-M-E but hadn't come up with anything better than a spell about the weather.

"Oh, there are so many possibilities," Mrs. Cicely

began. "I have an issue of *Spellbound Monthly* somewhere. . . ."

"Mr. Bishop has offered to help me and Trina prepare. Tomorrow, after school, during our magic lessons."

Mr. Bishop was B's English teacher, but when B visited him after class for extra study help, the tutoring didn't involve literature, or essays, or grammar. It involved potions, and spells, and magical travel to wonderful places. Lucky for B, she didn't need extra help in English. It was already her best subject.

"Make sure you make good use of your lesson time, then," Mrs. Cicely said. "Mr. Bishop can really help you out."

"Help out with what?" Mr. Cicely appeared in the doorway and set down his laptop bag. He smelled, as always, like a walking, talking cup of cocoa. It wasn't possible to work at the Enchanted Chocolates factory all day long and not have a little of it rub off.

"We were just discussing Friday's Young Witch Competition," Mrs. Cicely said.

"Ah." He sat down and kicked off his shoes. "B will clobber everyone else. I know she will. It runs in the family."

"That's what Geo . . ." B bit her lip. She almost let it slip that George knew about B's magic! It was a major rule of the Magical Rhyming Society to never let any nonwitches know about the existence of magic.

"Hm? What was that?"

"Uh . . ." B couldn't think of what to say.

"Now, Felix," B's mom said. "Hands off that guacamole. And B isn't going to 'clobber' anyone. That's *not* what the Young Witch Competition is about."

Mr. Cicely abandoned the guacamole and went for the cheese sauce instead. " 'Course not. 'Course not. Not about competition. It's about . . . er . . . teamwork."

"It's about learning," his wife corrected him. "And doing your best. So long as B works hard and tries hard, she'll have nothing to fear."

"Absolutely." Mr. Cicely scooped more guacamole when his wife's back was turned.

B was unconvinced.

Upstairs Trina's recorded voice belted out the chorus to "Swagger" for the third time straight, while Dawn's fancy footwork thumped with the beat. "Do your best" scarcely seemed like enough when your older sister was overloaded with both talent and magical skill.

"Dawn, come down for dinner!" Mrs. Cicely called up the stairs. "Dawn! Dawn! Oh, never mind." She wiped her hands on a dish towel. "We'll save her a plate. There's no stopping her practicing. She's one focused kid."

B kept her face aimed down at the table. There was that lecturing tone creeping into her mother's voice again.

"I'm sure that when *B* focuses on the Young Witch Competition, and decides what she wants to do, she'll put together a performance we'll be *very* proud of."

"Yeah." B swallowed a mouthful of dinner. It was

bad enough having to demonstrate her magical skills to an audience and panel of judges — that would inspire enough stage fright to render her clumsy and speechless for a week. But living up to Dawn was impossible, plain and simple.

"Why the long face, B?" her dad said.

"Oh, nothing," B said. "Pass the nachos, please."

Chapter 2

B entered the school building the next morning and wondered if she'd stumbled onto a Hollywood film set by mistake. Guys strummed unplugged electric guitars in front of their lockers. Two girls practiced their hip-hop dance while an eighth-grade boy belted out a rock ballad. Several cheer-leaders practiced their backflips down the corridors, nearly annihilating an innocent sixth-grade bystander. A pimply boy walked around with his head tilted back, balancing a bowling pin on the bridge of his nose.

B ducked her head down and dodged the crowd until she reached her locker. She didn't notice her friend approaching until Trina slid her arm through B's.

"Hey," B said, "what's going on around here?"

"Everyone's all wound up about the auditions," Trina said.

"But they're not until tomorrow."

"Doesn't matter," Trina replied. "Clifton Davro's coming. That's all anyone can talk about. This hubbub sort of reminds me of being on tour. All the road crew running around, the dancers and backup singers practicing all over the place . . ."

"You haven't considered doing the talent show, have you, Trina?"

B's friend shook her head. She looked each way to make sure no one could hear them. "Even if it didn't conflict with the Young Witch Competition, I wouldn't do it. I already get to perform on TV. It wouldn't be fair for me to take someone else's chance away."

"Yeah." B grinned. "And I wouldn't do it because I'm a chicken."

"You are not!"

B just shook her head and finished putting her things away in her locker.

"Anyway," Trina said, "I just saw Mr. Bishop. He said he's looking forward to us showing him what we've prepared for Friday night."

"Ugh," B groaned. "None of my ideas are any good. I'm so not ready."

"Well, don't worry," Trina said. "Mr. Bishop can help. You'll see."

The bell rang, and B and Trina headed toward their homerooms. A freshman ambled past them, letting out an earsplitting caterwaul.

"What was *that*?" B said.

Trina grinned. "Yodeling, I think."

All through art, history, and English classes, B's teachers battled bravely to keep everyone's attention, but B's classmates were far too interested in tomorrow's talent show auditions. Even Mr. Bishop, who usually kept his classes spellbound with his comical teaching and his rabbit-in-the-hat-style "magic" tricks, gave up trying to discuss vocabulary words from *Harriet the Spy*. He threw up his hands in despair, and assigned his students an extra essay on what they would do with the prize money if they won the national *You've Got It!* talent competition.

Lunch was in an uproar with everyone using every spare minute to practice their talents. After B, Trina, and George had eaten their food, they left the cafeteria early and headed down to the gym. George said he had something he wanted to show them.

The gym was empty when they arrived. George steered Trina and B toward a far corner, half-obscured by the collapsed bleachers. The overhead lights were off, so the room was only dimly lit by the overcast sky peeping through the skylights.

"Perfect," George said. "No one should see us here. I want you guys to tell me what you think of my act. I practiced for hours last night."

"Cool," Trina said. "What are you doing?"

George pulled a loop of climbing rope from his backpack. "First wrap me around and around with this, will you, B?"

B started tying George up.

"Careful! Don't cut off my circulation," George yelped. "Okay, Trina, would you take this padlock and fasten the clips of the rope together? Make sure the lock's behind my back."

B and Trina fussed with the rope and the lock until George was all trussed up.

"All right, ready? Here I go!" George began bouncing up and down, leaping high in the air and twisting. "I decided . . ." *jump* . . . "to be the bouncing . . ." *jump* . . . "joking . . ." *jump* . . . "escape artist." *Jump.*

"Oh, my goodness," Trina said. "That's quite a combination."

"I call myself . . ." *jump* . . . "Jumping . . ." *jump* . . . "Joking . . ." *jump* . . . "George."

"Let's hear some jokes, then," B said.

George kept on bouncing. "Well, I tried to think of some good ones," he said, "but I've been pretty *tied up* lately. Get it? *Tied up?*"

B and Trina groaned.

"I'm not the only jumper in my family, you know," George went on. "I've got a pair of twin brothers. The neighbors couldn't believe it when my parents named them both Jack. But how else could we call them *Jumping Jacks?*"

Trina and B exchanged a look. In spite of herself, B started to giggle.

"See? See? I'm making you laugh!" George said. "But these ropes aren't getting loose."

"Maybe that'll be enough for the judges," Trina said. "You look pretty funny, anyway."

"Help me get out of this, will you?" George said. "I guess I need to work more on the escape part of the act. Either that, or I need someone to tie me up more loosely."

B and Trina started tugging at George's rope.

"We'd better hurry," Trina said. "The bell's about to ring."

Just then, a movement from the opposite side of the gym caught B's eye. She turned just in time to see somebody duck behind the bleachers against the far wall.

"That dirty rotten sneak," B muttered to her friends. "He's spying on us."

"Who is?" George craned his neck to look.

"You might as well come out of hiding, Jason Jameson," B yelled across the gym. "We can see you."

Jason poked his freckled face out, then sauntered across the gym to where they stood.

"What's this little outfit, George?" Jason said, pointing to the rope. "Wait—let me guess. You're practicing your act. Are you going for the 'Biggest Idiot' award?"

"How could he," B fired back, "when you already hold the world heavyweight title?"

But Jason only smiled his nasty smile, showing all his braces. He tried to peek behind George's back, but George twisted and maneuvered to keep the padlock out of sight.

"Are you trying out, Jason?" Trina asked.

"I'm not just trying out," Jason said. "I'm going to dominate the competition. Nobody else will even *dare* compete after they see my act."

"Ooh, we're scared," B said.

"You should be, Bumblebee," Jason said. He was always calling B bug names. "After they've seen my act, the judges will probably cancel the rest of the auditions."

The bell rang. Other kids from their gym class

began pouring through the double doors. George scooched back out of sight and worked harder to escape from the rope.

"I pity you, George," Jason said. "Your act is so lame! The judges are gonna boo you right off the stage."

George's voice sounded worried. "He's right, isn't he?"

B's anger at Jason flared higher. "No way," she said. "Don't you dare let that rotten Jason make you feel bad about your act. It's . . . unique. You go for it. We're behind you all the way."

Chapter 3

B and Trina arrived together at Mr. Bishop's classroom a few minutes after the last bell rang.

"Come in, come in," he cried, beckoning toward them. "We have so much to cover today. Are you both ready with your special spells for Friday's Young Witch Competition?" He smiled. "Or has Clifton Davro—mania infected you, too?"

"Not me," B said. "Can you see me on a TV talent show? No, thanks."

"Me neither," Trina said. "I've met Cliff Davro a bunch of times. I'm much more interested in the magical competition. I've been working hard on my spell."

B looked down at her shoes. She'd been working hard, too. She'd stayed up late the night before, brainstorming and practicing different ideas. But none of them had worked out.

"Let's see it, then," Mr. Bishop said. "Show us what you've got."

"You first, Trina," B said.

Trina removed the treble-clef-shaped charm necklace Mr. Bishop had made for her. Trina's magic was different, too. Trina *sang* her rhyming spells in order to create magic. Without the treble-clef amulet, anything she sang made magic happen — a dangerous problem for a pop star! But now Trina wanted her singing magic to work. She planted her feet, threw back her shoulders, and took a deep breath. Her rich singing voice filled the classroom as she sang her spell for Mr. Bishop.

"For you, compose a melody;
Let magic make the harmony
And match the music perfectly
To what you love to hear.
Lilting lyrics reach down deep,
Make memories you'll want to keep.

A song to soothe you, help you sleep
While picture-dreams appear."

"Wow," B said. "That was so pretty."

"Wait," Trina whispered. "Listen."

At first it sounded like it came from far away, but gradually the sound swelled. It felt as if there was a live acoustic band playing right here in the classroom, with a virtuoso guitarist picking out the intricate chords and runs of a lively yet gentle song. The guitarist was soon joined by a mandolin, a fiddle, and a flute. The song had a folksy feel to it, but it was the kind that anyone would like. Each movement in the music sent waves of color shimmering up in the air, like drifting silk scarves, in front of Mr. Bishop. The images changed into an oceanfront scene, and then a field of grasses and wildflowers. B realized she was swaying back and forth to the tune.

Then an invisible lead vocalist, a woman, began to sing.

"Do you remember
Far, far away,

Do you remember

Our Summer's Eve day?"

A woman's face appeared. She had kind eyes and long, wavy brown hair, and she gazed fondly at Mr. Bishop. His eyes widened, and his face turned red. B felt a twinge of guilt, watching him, but she was too amazed and curious to stop.

"I still remember.

I can't forget

Our walk on the dunes.

My heart is there yet."

The music circled to a close, and the magical images faded. Mr. Bishop wiped his eye with a fingertip. He and B clapped enthusiastically.

"Wow, Trina," he said. "That was . . . unexpected."

"It was amazing!" B cried. "That song was so beautiful! And the pictures . . . so romantic . . . It's like Mr. Bishop's own special music video."

Trina blushed. "Thanks." She watched Mr. Bishop nervously. "Did it work? I mean, was the song . . . something you would like?"

Mr. Bishop rested his hand on Trina's shoulder. "Maybe a little too much. It reminded me of a band my friends and I formed in college. We used to play that kind of music."

Trina smiled, looking like she was trying not to make it *too* big. B could tell she was really pleased.

"You're next, B," Mr. Bishop said, and all the pleasure of Trina's spell evaporated.

"I don't have anything even close to that," B began. "I've tried lots of things, but I can't even think of a good idea. The best I could come up with last night was a cleanup spell for a messy bedroom, but I guess clean bedrooms aren't my thing." She grinned. "With or without magic." Her mother would attest to that.

"The best magic comes from our unique talents," Mr. Bishop said. "Try to think about what's unique about you."

"That's easy," Trina said. "I've never heard of another *spelling* witch. I mean, one who spells *words* in order to cast spells."

B sighed. "So, what should I do? Conjure up a

dictionary? Being able to spell words is no special skill. People's computers can do it for them."

Mr. Bishop twisted the tip of his shiny black goatee. "Tsk, tsk! How many of my English lectures have you sat through, and you think the most magical thing about words is how they're spelled? Think, B! Words are wondrously powerful! What else can you do with them?"

"Me?"

"Anybody."

B hated trick questions, and this felt like one. Mr. Bishop clearly had a specific answer he wanted, and B had no idea what it was. "You, er, talk using words," she said, "and write with them."

Mr. Bishop nodded. "Yes, yes. But what? Not just grocery lists and to-do lists. What can you tell or write with your words?"

B's gaze fell on a stack of books piled next to Mozart's cage. Mozart, the class hamster, lived in a tank on the windowsill in between the pencil sharpener and the class collection of paperback copies of *Where the Red Fern Grows*.

"Stories," B said. "Words can be shaped into stories."

"Exactly!" Mr. Bishop rubbed his hands together. "Trina came up with a songwriting spell, which, frankly, is pretty advanced magic. You could try a storytelling spell, couldn't you, B?"

B concentrated hard. This was one of the big problems with spelling words to perform magic. You only got a word or two. Rhyming and singing witches could describe what they wanted in much better detail. B had to focus hard to make her words produce the right results. Sometimes, even when she thought she'd focused perfectly, the spell still came out wonky.

"S-T-O-R-Y," she said, thinking hard about Mr. Bishop, stories, storytellers, and happy endings.

A gust of wind swept slowly through the room, ruffling the pages of books on desks, and even levitating a few paperbacks off the shelves. B watched nervously. What was going on?

"Once up on a time . . ." a voice began.

B breathed a sigh of relief. *It worked!* The voice

had a cool British accent. Trina squealed and gave B a high five.

"... there lived a family of giants."

Giants? Well, why not? Mr. Bishop's smile stretched from ear to ear.

"They lived in a cave in the side of a mountain and ate schoolteachers for breakfast, lunch, and supper each day."

Mr. Bishop laughed out loud, but B grew nervous. This wasn't the kind of story she had in mind at all!

"Their favorite kind of schoolteacher to eat was the kind that was also a witch. One day, the mother of the giant family, Mama Murgatroyd, got out her big copper kettle and began sharpening her chopping knives. 'Today's the day,' she told her big son Earl, 'that we'll go and hunt ourselves down a nice, plump ...'"

"S-T-O-P," B said, and flopped into the desk she used for English. "Never mind. That was horrible."

"What are you talking about?" Mr. Bishop asked. "I loved it! It had all the makings of a classic. Of course, if there are any little kids in the audience, they might be traumatized. . . ."

"You just need more practice. That's all," Trina said. "That was only your first time trying. You should have heard my first song spells! The beat was off, and the instruments were out of tune."

"Thanks for the idea," B said. "I'll definitely keep practicing." She shouldered her backpack. "I just hope there's time to make it come together before Friday."

Because if there isn't, B thought, *then the only thing I'll want to perform on Friday is a disappearing act.*

Chapter 4

The next day, trucks and vans full of film equipment filled the driveway in front of B's school. People B had never seen before swarmed the campus, running in and out with lengths of cable, makeup bags, extension cords, and big black boxes of lighting and sound equipment. B had to admit, it was pretty exciting. She found herself hoping for a glimpse of Clifton Davro.

When the bell rang at the end of the day, the competitors auditioning for the talent show lined up outside the auditorium. Kids of all ages from all over the city had come to try out. The line was snaking out the front door of the school. Dawn stood near the front of the line, flexing and stretching her leg muscles to get ready for her dance. She was all decked out in her dance costume, a pair of black jeans and a matching black T-shirt with "DIVA" in big white letters across the chest, and, capping it all off, giant hoop earrings and a pink hat cocked over a sleek blond ponytail.

"Good luck, Dawn," B said. "You look great. I love your costume."

Dawn gave B's arm a nervous squeeze. "Let's just hope I can remember all my moves."

George appeared farther back in the line, jostling a bag full of rope, locks, and other props. Trina showed up with her jacket and backpack, ready to leave. She thumped George on the back for good luck.

"Break a leg, George," Trina said.

"I just might," he said, "if I can't get myself untangled in time. I've got bruises all over from falling when I practiced."

"You'll be great," B said. "They'll love you. I really wish I could come watch your audition."

George shook his head. "The auditions are closed to the public. Judges and contestants only, this time around. That's what it says."

"I'd better get going," Trina said. "I promised my grandma I'd come straight home and practice for my . . . for, er, Friday's thing." She winked at B. "What are you up to?"

B felt that dread creep into her stomach — the familiar one that appeared whenever the Young Witch Competition was mentioned. "I . . . I need to practice today, too," she said. "I guess I'll stop by and see if Mr. Bishop is still here. Maybe he can give me some more tips."

With one last wave to Dawn and to George, B headed off to find Mr. Bishop. But when she reached his classroom, it was empty.

She sat in her usual seat near the window. Her gaze fell on a row of paperback novels standing on one of the shelves by the window. She picked up a few and looked at their covers. *The Last of the Mohicans. Gone with the Wind.* Mr. Bishop read *everything.*

Then she got an idea. Maybe her storytelling spell needed more guidance. Maybe she should think more about *genre*, or the kind of story she wanted to hear.

"W-E-S-T-E-R-N," she said.

Something settled on her head. The cactus on the windowsill had transformed into a ten-gallon Stetson cowboy hat!

A storytelling voice filled the room, but this time it had a cowboy drawl. "Howdy, pardner," it said. "Rassel them dogies up and get 'em out to pasture before the dinner gong."

"That doesn't make any sense at all," B said. "S-T-O-P. I never did like Westerns, and my spell could probably tell." She took a deep breath. "R-O-M-A-N-C-E."

To B's surprise, the cowboy hat floated to her desk and transformed into a cheerleader's pompom. The storytelling voice started, this time in dreamy tones. "Trevor lifted off his football helmet and gazed at Mandy. He had grease marks under his beautiful, deep blue eyes. Even after a grueling game against the Rudgertown Raiders, he was the most gorgeous guy she'd ever seen — and she'd cheered varsity three years straight.

" 'Who's taking you to the homecoming dance?' he asked.

"Mandy giggled and said, 'You are, silly.' "

"Yuck!" B said. "Stop, S-T-O-P, stop!" The pom-pom vanished. She was glad no one was around to hear those embarrassing story attempts. The Young Witch Competition was just three days away, and B was nowhere near ready. She sighed and sank down into a chair.

A movement near the window caught her eye. It was Mozart, standing on his hind legs in his tank and waving frantically to B. She opened the lid to his tank and lifted him out. B and Mozart had shared quite a few adventures since B found her spelling magic. She always had a soft spot for the cheeky little furball.

He snuffled around in the palm of her hand, then gazed at her, his whiskers twitching, his beady eyes shining.

"What is it, fella?" she said.

Mozart blinked at her. His meaning was obvious.

"I really shouldn't make you talk," B said. "Mr. Bishop wouldn't like it."

Mozart blinked again.

"Oh, okay, just for a minute," B said. "S-P-E-A-K."

"Phew! It's about time, missy. I've been waving at you for days but do you notice the lonely hamster? Noooo!"

"Hiya, Mozart," B said, grinning. "It's nice to see you, too."

Mozart jumped up and down in B's hand. "I've been stuck in that box all week, listening to kids yammering about the TV people and the talent show. Lemme go see it, will ya? I could be a star."

"Holy cats, Mozart, do you realize how dangerous that would be?"

The hamster twitched his whiskers at her. "C'mon, missy, don't *you* realize how *boring* it is to live in a cage and watch all the fun pass you by? The kids come; the kids go. You smell their lunch on their fingers when they come back from eating, and all you get is hamster chow. You hear them talk about cool things they do, but all you can do is dig in sawdust and run on your wheel." He thumped his tiny paw on his fluffy chest. "I've got dreams! I was made for better things! I've got as much talent in my little finger" — he held up his nearly microscopic claw — "as that nasty freckle-face boy has in his whole body."

"Jason Jameson?" B said. "That's a fact. I'd pick you any day over him."

"That's not saying much." He blinked at her once more. "Pretty please, missy? Just one little peek at the talent show. That's all I ask."

B hesitated. Mozart had a point. Didn't he? She would hate to be stuck in a tank, missing out on everything. What could go wrong?

A lot, actually. But, still . . . B *really* wanted to watch George and Dawn audition. Her magical practice sure wasn't making any progress. She'd have to be stealthy and absolutely quiet.

"You've got to promise me you won't run off or cause any trouble," B said.

"Hamster's honor," Mozart said.

"And you'll keep quiet?"

"Quiet as a mouse," Mozart said, "though where that saying came from, I don't know, because the mice I know, you can't get a word in edgewise around them. Talk your head off, a mouse will. I'm more the strong, silent type."

B grinned. "Is that so? Well, come on, Mozart. Let's check out that talent show."

Chapter 5

All the doors to the auditorium were locked. Peeking through a crack between one set of doors, B could barely make out the aspiring contestants seated in the front half of the auditorium, and a singer clutching a microphone on the stage. How could she get in without attracting attention? Her transportation spell didn't always work as well as she'd like. There was usually no telling where she'd land. And she didn't want to sit in the audience and get mistaken for a contestant — that would be awful! She needed a place to watch that was completely inconspicuous.

Carefully, soundlessly, she tugged on a backstage door, but it, too, was locked. She checked from side to side to make sure no one was watching, then spelled, "U-N-L-O-C-K." The bolt slid aside and the handle turned gently when she tried it. *Good thing I'd never be a thief,* B thought, suppressing a little smile.

She slipped inside. At first B couldn't see anything past the dozens of curtains in the wings, blocking her view. She tiptoed forward, still holding Mozart cupped in her palm, until she had a glimpse of the stage. B peeked into the auditorium and saw rows and rows of kids all waiting their turn to audition. A girl in a tutu was bowing, and the judges, seated behind a long table at the far side of the stage, clapped halfheartedly. The man seated at the middle of the table wore sunglasses and a leather jacket, and his hair was all spiky. It was Clifton Davro!

As the ballerina left the stage, Clifton Davro conferred with Ms. Andrews, the school drama teacher, who seemed to be telling him about the next contestant as she took the stage. B noticed Ms. Andrews's cheeks were pinker than usual, especially when Clifton Davro leaned closer. Two other judges sat at the table, one on either side of Clifton Davro and Ms. Andrews, but B didn't recognize either of them.

B scooched in closer. "Dawn Cicely," an announcer called. "Let's see if *You've Got It!*"

Dawn! B felt a flutter of sympathetic nerves for her sister. But Dawn strode out onto the stage like she was born there. She struck a pose with one leg crossed over the other as she waited for her music to start, one hand tipping the brim of her pink hat low over her forehead. She looked like a star, and her act hadn't even started!

The sound system guys seemed to be having a hard time finding the music. Dawn waited, keeping her pose straight.

"What's the matter?" B heard Jason Jameson yelling loud and clear from the auditorium. "Waiting in line for the bathroom? Try the boys' room. There's never a line."

Why didn't they disqualify him then and there? B couldn't believe they let people heckle like that.

But Dawn didn't bat an eyelash. For all anyone could tell, she'd never even heard.

The opening beats of "Swagger" filled the auditorium, and Dawn launched into a perfect twirl. B had to admit, it was pretty neat watching her sister dancing like a pro to a song sung by one of her best friends for a TV judging panel.

"That's my sister, Mozart," B whispered. "Isn't she great?"

"Sure, yeah, she's got some moves," Mozart said.

Dawn didn't miss a single step. Even B, who had watched Dawn's recitals for years, was impressed. Her sister was electric today. B could tell the judges and the audience agreed.

"Swagger" finished with Dawn doing a perfect break-dance spin on the stage. The audience erupted with applause, and B grinned. She couldn't clap while still holding Mozart, and of course she wasn't supposed to be there at all, so she kept quiet otherwise.

Clifton Davro jumped to his feet and raised his

sunglasses. "You've got it!" he yelled, giving Dawn a huge thumbs-up. Dawn blushed pinker than her hot-pink hat, bowed, and ran off the stage.

The announcer called for Frankie Hotchkiss, an awkward sixth-grader wearing suspenders and a red bowtie. B heard snickers of laughter run through the audience. Frankie heard them, too, but he faced the microphone with a grim sort of courage that made B vow to go out of her way to say hi to him from now on. She had a feeling she knew just how scared he was, and she had to hand it to him for trying anyway. His music began, and more kids laughed. It was a well-known song from a movie popular with little kids. Frankie opened his mouth and began to sing.

Then the laughing began in earnest. Frankie Hotchkiss might sound all right singing in the shower, but his was not a voice meant for show business. Jason Jameson's familiar, mean laugh rose above the others. B felt even more upset. Poor Frankie. It wasn't his fault he couldn't sing well. Jason had no business being cruel to him.

"Listen to the pork chop try to sing," Mozart squeaked. "He sounds like a pencil sharpener chewing through a metal pen."

"Hush, Mozart," B hissed. "No talking! You'll get us in trouble."

"You're right," Mozart said. "He sounds more like a school bus driving away with its parking brake still on."

"Quiet! And stop being mean, too. One more peep out of you, and I'm taking you back to your tank."

"Aww, you wouldn't do that to your old pal Mozart, would you? I've only heard one song so far, and this rotten kid singer doesn't count."

"Amazing!" said a voice behind her.

B felt a chill of terror run down her spine. She looked up to see a tall woman peering down at her. She wore a headset and carried a clipboard, and her steel gray hair was coiled up in a tight bun. *I'm in big trouble*, B thought. Then she saw where the woman's eyes were fixed. *It's worse than I thought!* The woman couldn't take her eyes off Mozart!

"I could have sworn that gerbil was actually talking!" the woman said.

"Hamster," B said, her stomach sinking.

"You're quite the little ventriloquist. My name's Nancy. I'm the director of the show," the woman said. "You shouldn't be back here, you know. You should be in the audience with the other contestants. What's your name? Where are you on the list?"

"My name's Beatrix Cicely, but I'm not on the list," B began. "I'm just . . ."

"Well, we'll fix that," Nancy said. "Let's not wait. This act is about to finish, and we'll get you right on. Cliff's gonna love you." She frowned. "But you haven't got a costume. Hmm." She snapped her fingers. "I know! Where's that trunk . . . ?" She reached around a curtain and pulled out a tall silk top hat. Without a word, she clapped it onto B's head.

"Nice hat," Mozart said.

Frankie's song ended, and he bowed his head to acknowledge the trickle of applause that came his way. His face shone with sweat, but B was too terrified to pity Frankie Hotchkiss now.

"Thank you, er, Frankie, for that number," Clifton Davro said. "You have a unique voice, and you should definitely, um, keep plugging away at your practicing."

Frankie nodded. "Thank you, sir."

"It's not quite the tone we're looking for at *You've Got It!*" Davro said with a pleasant smile, "but keep your chin up and try again, all right?"

Frankie nodded and walked off the stage, looking relieved.

"Our next act is Jason —" the announcer began, but Nancy dragged B out onto the stage.

"Hold up a sec," she said. "Slight change in schedule. Our next act is Miss Beatrix Cicely, a ventriloquist, performing with her amazing 'talking' hamster!"

Chapter 6

"A ventriloquist?" Clifton Davro said. "We've never had one of those."

"As a matter of fact—" B said, but Nancy cut her off.

"You have got to see this; she's incredible!"

B turned to Nancy and pleaded, "Ma'am, I can't do this!"

The director leaned closer and whispered back, "Sure you can, honey. Don't be shy. Just do what you showed me backstage. They'll be crazy about you." She patted B on the shoulder and walked away, her high heels clicking on the wooden floor.

B felt the silence of the audience and all eyes on her. This must be a nightmare. B closed her eyes and opened them again, but nothing had changed.

What could she do? What if someone figured out that B wasn't really throwing her voice? She'd blow the secret of witches existing, not just to her entire school, but maybe even on national television!

She had to get out of there. She was about to just plain bolt for the wings, when a stagehand moved Frankie's microphone right over to where B stood, still holding Mozart.

"Nice hat," Clifton Davro said. "All right, then, Miss . . . What was it?"

"Beatrix," Nancy called from the wings.

"All right, then, Miss Beatrix, show us what you've got." The celebrity talent judge leaned back in his chair and folded his arms behind his head.

B closed her eyes and leaned toward the microphone. "I'm really sorry," she began, but jumped at the echo of her voice playing back at her through the speakers. "There's been a mix-up, and . . ."

"Darn right!" Jason's voice yelled from the audience. "It was a big mix-up letting you in here. People with *real* talent are waiting to go on."

"Oh, yeah?" Mozart cried. "Zat you, Freckle Face? You're mixed up in the *head*!" The microphone caught his squeaky voice and blared it through the auditorium. A ripple of surprise ran through the crowd.

B couldn't help smiling, just a little. "Not now, Mozart, okay? Let's go."

"Wait a second," Mozart said, sniffing the microphone. "Does this thingamabob make it so all you kids out there can hear me?"

"*Yes!*" the audience yelled.

"All righty, then." Mozart rubbed his paws together. "Listen up, cuz I've got a long list of stuff I've been wanting to tell you bozos, and now you're gonna hear it."

B wished she could disappear. But that would draw even more attention to her magic than a talking hamster. How, oh, *how* did she always get into such trouble? B saw the judges grinning and whispering to one another. Mozart was a hit.

"Did you know that a middle school hamster sees about fifteen kids a day pick their noses when they think no one's looking? Ain't no gold up there, folks, no matter how you dig!"

The audience laughed.

"And there's usually a kid or two who doesn't care if anyone's looking or not. Not gonna be named Peter Popular, if you know what I mean."

More laughter.

"And don't get me started on the pickers and eaters!" Mozart squeaked, waving his little paws high. "People: I got something to say to you. Three words. Wait. For. Lunch!"

The audience was howling now, with a bunch of "Eeew, gross" remarks mixed in. No doubt about it. Mozart was a hit.

If they thought B was a ventriloquist, she might as well play the part—and get off the stage as quickly as she could.

"Now, Mozart," she began. "Isn't it time for your nap?"

"Naps are for sissies," Mozart retorted. "Speaking of lunch, see these teeth? Nature made these teeth to chew through anything! No more of the dusty kibble food, okay? A carrot now and then wouldn't hurt anybody. Or one of those chocolate bar thingies I see you sneak at your desks when the teacher's not looking. Think of the hamster now and then, eh?"

"That's enough, Mozart," B said. "We've taken too much of their time. Let's go back to your tank."

"You kidding? I'm not gonna take no stinking nap! This here's a talent show, and I'm not leaving till I show my talent, see? Now, listen up, folks. They don't call me Mozart for nothing."

Oh, no. What next? B glanced sideways to see the judges watching, enjoying Mozart's show with big grins on their faces.

"I got a song for ya," Mozart said. "You know that Elvis guy? Well, my version is called 'Fish Tank Rock.' I'm not a fish, but 'Hamster Tank Rock' didn't fit the beat so good."

And without missing a beat, Mozart launched into his song, bopping from side to side and swinging his paws in the air.

"The hamster threw a party in the old fish tank,
But no one'd cleaned his sawdust so the party
    stank.
The rabbits from the science room brought
    carrot sticks,
You should've seen the hamster's crazy dancing
    tricks,
Let's rock! Everybody, let's rock.
Everybody in the sixth-grade block,
They was dancing to the Fish Tank Rock!
Yeah!"

He waved his paws in the air for the finale, Broadway-style.

B was speechless.

But not Clifton Davro.

"Incredible!" he yelled. B looked to see him rise from his seat and give her a double thumbs-up. "Fantastic, stupendous, incredible! You've got it, Beatrix!"

Oh, no! Had she just accidentally landed herself a spot in the finals?

The audience rose to their feet and cheered. Jason Jameson roared out a big "Boo!" but he was drowned out by the applause. B bowed, which made her tall hat fall to the floor. She scooped it up and ran off the stage into the wings . . .

. . . and ran straight into a scowling, fuming Dawn.

Chapter 7

"Nice act, B," Dawn said, her arms folded across her chest. "How come you never mentioned at home that you were planning to enter the competition? And *jeopardize the witching world* in the process?"

"Dawn, you have to believe me, I didn't mean to—"

"How can you say you didn't mean to, when there you were, on the stage with a top hat and a talking hamster? That kind of thing doesn't happen by accident!"

"But that's just it!" B said. "It *was* an accident. I was just watching, when—"

"I don't have time to listen to this," Dawn

interrupted again. "Hope you're proud of yourself, B." She spun on her heel and left.

"Geez Louise," Mozart said. "*Somebody* needs a sense of humor."

B glared at the troublemaking hamster. "I think we've heard enough from you today. S-P-E-E-C-H-L-E-S-S." Mozart blinked at her disapprovingly, then snuffled around her palm.

B took a deep breath. She felt shaky all over. It was bad enough being out there on the stage in front of half the school. Now her big sister was furious with her. Her parents were sure to hear about this, and then she'd be in even bigger trouble.

She turned to leave the stage through the back door, then paused. The announcer had called the next act, but she hadn't heard the name. She peeped through the curtains.

It was Jason Jameson, looking smug as usual.

In spite of herself, B wondered what Jason would do, after all that bragging.

"Ladies and gentlemen," he said. "I present

to you feats of escape that will blow your imagination!"

Feats of escape? What?

He's stolen George's act!

Somehow Jason had come up with a fancy wooden cupboard, decorated with shiny moons and stars. B groaned. He had taken George's idea — and *improved* it.

"Behold: a straitjacket and regulation police handcuffs. May I have a volunteer from the audience to assist me? Jenny, how about you?"

B gritted her teeth. Jenny Springbranch was always fawning over Jason. B was sure she was no random volunteer. She'd probably be slipping Jason the keys to his handcuffs.

"Jenny, do these objects appear to be tampered with in any way?"

Jenny shook her head. "No, Mr. Jameson. They look perfectly normal."

Mr. Jameson! Jumping jinxes. Who did she think she was kidding?

"And how about this cupboard? Will you

investigate it for the audience and make sure it's solid and intact?"

Deep, sinister music began to play. The effect was definitely suspenseful.

"Now, Jenny, will you assist me in getting into this straitjacket and fastening the handcuffs on tight behind my back? Make sure there's no way for me to escape."

Jenny secured Jason into his bindings, showing the audience how tightly he was bound. He entered the cupboard, and she shut and locked the door.

"Everyone, count with me," Jenny cried. "Ten, nine, eight . . ."

The audience joined in. The auditorium boomed with each chanted number.

"Four, three, two . . ."

B held her breath. On the count of one, Jason burst from the cupboard, completely free from his handcuffs and his jacket. He took a flamboyant bow, and the audience went wild.

Clifton Davro shoved his shades down the bridge of his nose. "You've got it, kid," he said. "I've got a feeling we'll see you in a couple of days."

Jason punched the air with his fist, then bowed once more. Jenny Springbranch helped him carry his stuff off the stage.

B drooped. Poor George! He must be devastated right now. Mozart climbed up B's arm and onto her shoulder, as if he wanted a better look.

"And now, for our last contestant," the announcer said. "George Fitzsimmons!"

George hopped onto the stage, wrapped from head to toe in rope and padlocks. His face was glum but determined. He had apparently abandoned his thought of telling jokes while he did his escape act. B figured that was probably just as well. But after Jason's spectacular performance, no one seemed to pay attention to George. Even the judges were whispering among themselves and writing on their notepads. They barely even looked at him.

George struggled on and on with his rope. Finally Clifton Davro looked at his watch.

"Time's up, son," he said in a kindly voice. "Thanks for showing us your act. It's got potential. You just need to practice escaping faster."

George stopped wriggling, nodded, and shuffled off the stage. Nancy appeared by the scoring table and collected sheets from all the judges, then hurried back offstage near where B stood to tally her results. B hid behind a curtain to watch. Music played from the speakers to pass the time while the votes were counted.

Nancy rose to take the results back to where the judges waited. Just then, her cell phone beeped. She set her clipboard back down and flipped open her phone. "Hi. What's up? Yeah, I can't really talk right now. I'm . . . Okay. Give me one sec." She looked both ways, then slipped through the backstage door and out into the hallway.

B couldn't help herself. She tiptoed to the table to look at the clipboard. There in black and white were the results — the names of the contestants who would progress to the final round and compete against winners from nearby cities for the coveted place on the television show. Nancy had listed the top vote-getters in order:

Beatrix

Jason

Dawn

B had won the first round!

Chapter 8

I won the talent show, and I didn't even mean to enter.

B let the thought sink in.

I even beat Dawn.

Jumping jinxes. This couldn't be happening.

But Dawn had earned her spot through talent and lots of hard work. B's accidental gig was based solely on magic — that, and Mozart's crazy personality. She had to put a stop to this somehow.

"Nancy? You still back there?" It was Clifton Davro's voice. At any second the director would return from her phone call. There was only one thing to do.

"C-H-A-N-G-E," she whispered, staring at her name on the page. B's name faded from view as though an invisible hand had scrubbed it out with an eraser, stroke by stroke. But before a new name could appear, the door opened, and Nancy ran back through, looking flustered. B retreated out of sight just in time. Nancy snatched the clipboard off the table and hurried back out to the microphone.

"Each of you kids did a great job, and you should be very proud of yourselves for having the courage to audition," she said. "Let's have a big round of applause for all our contestants!"

Everyone clapped, then stopped, eager to hear the results.

"I'm pleased to announce our winners," she said. "These are the names of the contestants who will represent your city on Friday night, where they'll compete with the winners from nearby cities for just one place on our live TV show. When I call your name, please come up onstage. The contestants who will be progressing are . . ." There was a drumroll sound, then a pause while Nancy looked confused. She shrugged and announced, "Jason Jameson and Dawn Cicely!"

Jason came running up to the stage, shaking his hands over his head like a boxing champion. Dawn followed after, with several of her high school friends cheering for her. They stood side by side and bowed to the audience.

Clifton Davro peered over the top of his shades. "Um, Nancy, are you sure you read the right names?"

Nancy checked her clipboard.

"That's right, Cliff," she said. "According to the point scores you judges gave, these are our winners."

Clifton Davro shot a confused look at his fellow judges, then smiled and said, "Well, then, congratulations! You did a fantastic job, and you're going on to Friday's finals. The best act from that will be on the TV show. See you then. That's a wrap." He rose and turned to leave.

B tiptoed away quickly, in case any of the judges or contestants left by the stage door near where she stood. She needed to get Mozart back to his cage.

When she left Mr. Bishop's room after refreshing Mozart's water, she headed for George's locker. She found him there, stuffing his jumbled escapologist ropes and padlocks inside without really looking at what he was doing.

"Hey, George," B said. "I thought you did great."

"Ha." George didn't look up. "I was a disaster."

"No, you weren't. It was a really original idea. It was only because Jason swiped it from you that it didn't go over so well."

George closed his locker. "I looked like an idiot. Where did Jason get his hands on a straitjacket, anyway? And that cupboard? Man!"

"He wasn't so impressive," B said. "There's no way Jenny Springbranch was just a volunteer. She probably slipped him the keys to his handcuffs. I don't see why the judges chose him as the winner."

George looked at B for the first time since she'd shown up, but he still wasn't smiling. "Your act was better than his," he said. "How come you didn't tell me you were entering the competition?"

"I wasn't planning to. I . . ."

George wiped his glasses on his sweatshirt. "Well, it doesn't matter. You did great."

They left the school with their backpacks and started walking home. B explained everything that had happened, from Mozart begging to see the auditions to Nancy giving her the hat.

George laughed at last. "This could only happen to you, B."

"And then when Mozart started singing, I just wanted to disappear."

"That song was hilarious," George said. "But the best part by far was Mozart telling off Jason. Mozart deserves to win the contest."

"Next time we have a conversation — which, if I have any sense, won't be anytime soon — I'll be sure to tell him."

Chapter 9

"If everyone is in their groups, please begin to discuss the list of questions about *Harriet the Spy*. I'll be back in a minute."

Mr. Bishop stepped outside his classroom. Everyone had moved their desks into groups. B, George, and Jamal formed one, while Jason, Trina, and Jenny Springbranch formed the group next to them.

"Question one," George said. "'What was Harriet's favorite kind of sandwich?'"

"Um, cheese," Jason said. "Like how I'm the big cheese in the talent show."

"Excuse me, Jason," B said, "but the answer is tomato. And you're supposed to discuss the book with *your* group. So if you've got to barge in and brag, at least get the answer right."

Trina read the next question aloud. "'Why do you think Harriet liked to go spying?'"

"To watch me win the school talent show!" Jason said, snickering.

Trina and B exchanged annoyed glances.

"You're really pathetic, you know that, Jason?" Jamal said.

"I'm sorry. I didn't hear you," Jason replied. "Did you say I'm really fantastic? Because I already knew that. And on Friday, the judges are going to find out for themselves. And then, I'm on TV, baby!"

"We're supposed to be working, Jason," Trina said.

"Did anybody else here make it to Friday's finals?" Jason said, with a pretend-innocent face. "You tried out, didn't you, George? Oh, right, you had that lame escape act with the rope. Don't know why you bothered. You tried out, too, didn't you, Beeswax? Oh, wait, no. It was the *hamster* that auditioned. If it wasn't for you, the hamster would have won!"

Jason laughed triumphantly.

"So the hamster is better than you?" George said. "Wow. Must stink to be beaten by a rodent."

Jason scowled.

For a second B regretted changing her name on the winner's list. It would have been so sweet to see Jason's face after B came out on top. Then she reminded herself how many other disasters that would have caused.

"B's sister made the finals," George said. "She came up with her *own* act. Not a rip-off of someone else's."

Mr. Bishop came back in the room, and that settled Jason down for the rest of the class period. But during lunch, B, Trina, and George sat down together just in time to see Jason parading out from the lunch line, followed by a string of giggling girls.

"What on earth?" Trina asked. "Look! That's not what I think it is, is it?"

Sure enough, Jason sat down, whipped out a pen, and began signing autographs!

"I think I've lost my appetite," B said, pushing her lunch away.

"Look, he's charging a dollar for each autograph," Trina said. "I've never seen anyone so stuck-up. That kid is unbelievable."

"I can't believe anyone would pay a buck for a piece of paper Jason touched," B said. "Blaugh. I'd pay a dollar *not* to."

George whipped out a sheet of paper from his notebook. "Here you go. That'll be a dollar, B."

B smiled. "Ha-ha. Very funny."

"Jason's ego was bad enough before this," Trina said. "Now it's dinosaur-size."

"So what else is new?" George said.

"I hope your sister clobbers him at the finals on Friday, B," Trina said. "I've heard a lot of people say her dance was amazing. Of course, she picked a great song!"

"I hope so, too," B said. She took a bite of her sandwich. "But she's still mad at me. She wouldn't believe me when I told her my Mozart act was an accident. I'm just lucky she never told Mom and Dad."

"She'll get over it," Trina said. "Hey, B, go with me to the M.R.S. this afternoon?"

"What for?"

Trina's eyes widened. "Madame Mel is hosting a review session — to help all of us prepare for tomorrow's competition."

B pushed her sandwich away again. Ah. She'd been trying to forget about that one. Now she really had no appetite.

"Oh, *that* meeting," B said, trying to sound relaxed. "Sure. I'll meet you at your locker."

B and Trina arrived at the Magical Rhyming Society just as the Young Witch Competition meeting was starting. They tiptoed through the doors to the tall, circular library and snuck into seats at the nearest table.

"Greetings, Trina, Beatrix," Madame Mellifluous said. "Nice of you to join us."

Shoot. So much for slipping in unnoticed.

Madame Mel, the Grande Mistress and Head Librarian of the Magical Rhyming Society, climbed onto a short pedestal and held out her arms, making the sleeves of her lavender robe flap like wings. Her robes were festooned from collar to hem with thousands of tinkling silver charms — visible proof of her countless magical triumphs throughout her career. Her purple spectacles sat perched on the tip of her long, skinny nose, and her powder blue hair was in a tight bun.

"Welcome, young witches, to the Magical Rhyming Society. I'm sure you've all been practicing for weeks and are ready and eager to show this illustrious society what you can do at tomorrow's competition."

B's stomach flopped. Why did it seem like every other witch here was full of confidence, whereas B felt none?

"I'm sure I need not mention to you bright young magical scholars the long and proud tradition of this competition." Madame Mel's keen eyes swept the room. "For over two hundred years, the Magical Rhyming Society has held this competition to recognize and promote the achievements of our young witches. It's even older than this grand building in which we sit."

B's eyes wandered to the tall, curved bookshelves lining the walls of the library. Glittering volumes inserted themselves into place, or whisked neatly off the shelves by magic, floating through the air to the hands of waiting librarians.

"Many of this society's most esteemed witches are listed on the roster of past winners," Madame Mel went on. "Rozmilda Runce was an early winner. Hugo Thistleweed first caught the notice of the M.R.S. at a Young Witch Competition." She coughed modestly. "Even I, myself, am proud to wear a prize charm from my own Young Witch Competition."

My sister, Dawn, won when she was eleven, B thought. *Does that mean Dawn will become a great and famous witch someday?* Even if Dawn was mad at her at the moment, B admired her big sister.

Up till now, the competition had been something B dreaded, something her parents nagged her to prepare for. Only here, listening to Madame Mel, did she realize how important it was to practice and develop her magic, to show the witching world what she could do.

Now B wanted to try. She only hoped it wasn't too late.

Chapter 10

"As you know, the competition is divided into three phases," Madame Mel said. "The first is Quickfire Questions. Each contestant will stand before the judges and answer three questions. Answers must be quick, thorough, and accurate. They will cover a variety of magical subjects including potions, charms, spell-casting, the Three High Dictums, witching history, and general magical knowledge. You will all do well on the questions, I'm sure."

Some of the witches at nearby tables looked like they weren't as convinced as Madame Mel.

"Next comes the Special Spell," she continued. "This is where you cast for us a spell of your own creation that showcases your unique magical flair. On Friday, judges will be most impressed by spells that show evidence of careful planning. And the last portion of the competition will be a potion exhibition. Any potions that result in foul smells or bodily injury to the judges will be disqualified."

The more Madame Mel talked, the more B's stomach felt like it did when she looped-the-loop on the MegaCoaster after helping George finish a bag of Enchanted Chock-o-Rocks. By the time orientation ended, the only spell B wanted to cast was one that would make herself disappear.

The next day at school, B and George stepped off the bus to even more film crew commotion. Now that contestants were coming from all the nearby cities, the number of technicians seemed to have tripled. Excitement was high, because the winner would perform on live network television. Students were drawn to the cameras like flies to melted slushies. Every time a cameraman looked through his viewfinder, he inevitably found kids staring back at him and sticking out their tongues or making faces.

Things were no different at lunchtime. It was

"breakfast for lunch" day, and the cafeteria smelled like sausages and pancakes when B, George, and Trina arrived in the cafeteria and found a film crew there, taking some footage of the lunchroom scene.

"What's this for?" George asked a man fiddling with the buttons on his camera. "You're not auditioning for talented eaters, are you?"

The man paused and turned to look at George. "Heh. You've got a good sense of humor," he said. "What's your name?"

"George."

"Listen, George," the man said. "I need to interview a kid about the show. It'll be part of a little intro segment. Why don't I interview you?"

George shoved his glasses up his nose. "Really? Me? Sure!"

"My name's Ed," the cameraman said. "Let me just get this configured right, and then we'll start. Got a few minutes?"

"You bet," George said. He turned to B and Trina and whispered, "I'm going to be on TV after all!"

B grinned.

Ed positioned George in a seat and trained the camera on him.

"So tell me, George, how does it feel to have Clifton Davro and the whole *You've Got It!* crew here at your school?"

Ed asked the question while still squinting into his camera. It took George a second to realize that it was his turn to talk.

"Oh, um, it's fantastic. Yeah, people are really excited about it." George looked to Ed for direction on what he should do next. When he didn't say anything, George went on. "Clifton Davro is completely awesome and his show is the best thing on TV!"

B smiled. George's second comment was sure to please the show's producers.

"Did you audition for the show?"

George hesitated. "I did audition, but I didn't make it past the first round. But I sure had fun trying!"

"Lots of people who miss out on the national show still go on to be successful," Ed said. "Keep on plugging!"

"It's okay," George said. "Some people have a talent for dancing or singing, but I'm best out on the soccer field."

"Good for you," Ed said. "That's a great sentiment for the show's viewers who might not have made it themselves. Thanks, George! Great sound bites."

George beamed.

"What are you up to, Ed?"

B turned to see Nancy, the show's director, behind them.

"Just taping some interviews to open this region's live show," Ed replied. "George here has been helping me out."

"Thanks, George," Nancy said.

B slid behind Trina and tried to make herself inconspicuous. She didn't want Nancy to remember her from her top-hat-and-hamster gig.

Then Jason Jameson popped up. "*I* think you should do an interview with the favorite contestant," Jason said in his most annoying, teacher's-pet voice.

Nancy frowned and looked around. "The

favorite? I don't see her here. What was her name? The pretty dancer — Dawn something."

Trina gave B's arm a squeeze. Apparently Nancy hadn't remembered Jason's face, which now looked like an angry thundercloud.

"I've got to get to the stage," Nancy said. "Let's get the rest of the cameras tested before we shoot." Ed followed Nancy out, giving George a thumbs-up as he went.

"That showed you," B said to Jason.

Jason scowled. "There's no way Dawn will win," he said. "It's going to be me. You'll see."

Chapter 11

B, Trina, and George finally ate their lunch, still talking about *You've Got It!*

"I still can't believe I was interviewed for a TV show," George said. He wadded up a piece of tinfoil and lobbed it into the trash. "Did you see that? Three point shot by George Fitzsimmons, Sound-Bite Star!"

B was glad for George. After yesterday's disastrous audition, he deserved a boost like this. But she couldn't get her mind off the look on Jason's face just a moment ago.

"Do you think Jason was just bragging?" B said. "When he said he was going to be the winner? 'You'll see'? It sounded to me like he had something up his sleeve."

"Knowing Jason, he probably does," said Trina. "He's always up to something."

"Look," George said. "He's going back into the kitchen with his backpack on. I wonder why."

They all looked at one another. "Let's go see," B said. "I've got a funny feeling about this."

"We can't just follow him," Trina said. "He'll see us, and then he'll stop doing . . . whatever it is he was planning on."

"I've got an idea," B said. "Let's go!"

They dumped their trash and exited the cafeteria, then stood in the hallway next to the kitchen, where the beginning of the lunch line formed. The halls were empty, since all the sixth-graders had already gone through the line.

"I'm going to make us smaller," B said, "so we can sneak in there and listen to what he's saying. We'll be like little mice."

"Um, B," Trina said nervously. "Remember how this didn't go so well last time? At the Enchanted Chocolates factory?"

Trina had a point. Last time they shrunk themselves, it took some fancy magical footwork to return Trina to her proper size. But B brushed her concern aside. "It'll work better this time," she said. "I learn from my mistakes." And, thinking hard about the three of them, she spelled, "M-I-N-I-A-T-U-R-E."

The hallway around them grew larger and larger, as they got smaller and smaller. When they stopped shrinking, B realized she was about the height of one of the small ceramic tiles on the wall. Awesome!

"B?" Trina said. "People call me Kat. They don't ever call me Mouse."

B grinned. "Good one, Trina. I . . ." She stopped when she'd taken a closer look at her friend.

She'd sprouted mouse ears and a tail! George, too.

B felt her own scalp, and, sure enough, poking out from her own head was a pair of mousey ears. A long tail swished behind her when she turned to look.

"At least it's only ears and a tail," B said, feeling sheepish. "Look at the bright side."

"I hope this doesn't last as long as the time you turned me into half-boy, half-zebra," George muttered.

"I'll fix it," B said. "But if we don't hurry, we'll miss whatever Jason's got planned. Let's go!"

They ran as fast as they could through the kitchen door and climbed into the base of a brass post supporting the cordon rope that marked off the flow of the lunch line. Surely no one would notice them there.

"Lunch was delicious today," Jason was saying. "Waffle day is one of my favorites."

"We served pancakes today," Mrs. Gillet, the cafeteria manager, said.

"Er, right," Jason said. "Um, when do you think you'll serve waffles next?"

"It'll be listed on the menu."

"Well, do you think you could check? Right now?"

B, George, and Trina exchanged glances. Jason was trying to get rid of her.

"We're all kind of busy here, getting ready for the seventh-grade lunch," Mrs. Gillet said.

Jason began to sniffle and rub his eyes. "I . . . I just . . . I just really like waffles. . . ." B and George and Trina gaped at one another. Crying? Nobody would buy that.

The cafeteria manager rolled her eyes. "Okay, okay, it's all right. Wait here a sec and I'll go look at the monthly menu." She wiped her hands on her apron and disappeared into the rear of the kitchen.

Jason's tears dried up immediately. He smiled, smug as anything, and popped behind the serving counter.

"What's he doing?" Trina peeped in a tiny voice.

"He's getting something off a shelf and stuffing it in his backpack," B said. "I can't see what it is, but he's taking two — no, three of them."

"Lousy thief," George muttered. "Why does he

need to go robbing a school cafeteria? What's he after, ketchup?"

"Ssh! Here he comes!" B hissed. Sure enough, at the sound of the cafeteria manager's returning footsteps, Jason bolted out from behind the corner and stood as if he hadn't budged an inch.

"Waffle day is two weeks from tomorrow," Mrs. Gillet said. B peered around the brass post for a closer look at Jason, in case she could get a view of his backpack.

Mrs. Gillet continued, "We'll be serving sausage links, hash browns, and — *aaaiiiiiieeeeee!*"

B jumped at the shrill, unexpected scream.

"Mice!" Mrs. Gillet screamed. "Right there!"

And she pointed a shaking finger toward where B and her friends were hiding.

Jason screamed and bolted out of the kitchen doors.

"Run!" B squeaked.

She, George, and Trina took off after Jason, but at four inches tall, three yards felt like a mile to all of them.

"Take *that*!" Mrs. Gillet jabbed her broom at them. The bristles brushed B's tail. But Mrs. Gillet swung with such force that she overbalanced and crashed onto her bottom.

B and her friends darted out the door and collapsed in a heap behind it, panting. Jason was long gone. B racked her brain to think of how to undo her spell. "N-O-R-M-A-L S-I-Z-E," she spelled. Nothing happened. "G-R-O-W." Trina's hair started to wave and lengthen, until it stretched down to her mouse-size waist!

Mrs. Gillet's loud voice echoed from within. B knew she didn't have any time to spare. *Think. Think!* She'd done this once before. But how? She needed to turn them back to their regular selves. Without any mouse parts.

Themselves. She pictured them in her mind. "K-A-T-R-I-N-A," she spelled. And, *voila!* Trina appeared in her normal size. No mouse ears, no tail.

Mrs. Gillet stuck her nose out the door. "Hi there, young lady," she said. "You haven't seen a handful of mice running around, have you?"

"Um, no, definitely not," Trina said.

"Well, if they're in my kitchen," she said, clutching her broom with white knuckles, "I'll find them!" And she disappeared back inside.

B knew she had better get everyone back to normal right away.

"G-E-O-R-G-E," she spelled. And *pop!* George sprang back to full size.

B didn't need much time. "B," she whispered. Then she felt herself stretch alarmingly tall and, quick as lightning, B was standing there next to her friends.

"Whew," B said. But she was still no closer to finding out what Jason was up to.

That afternoon at home, B worked on her potion for the Young Witch Competition. It was only a day away, and B knew she had a lot of work left to do before she'd be ready. She decided that her bedroom would be a good place to try something like Dawn's makeover spell, brewing it as a potion. That was where she had the most beauty ingredients available, though B didn't have anywhere near as much stuff as Dawn did — nail polish and earrings and cool shoes and hair clips. But she gathered together what she could find.

First she combined a gold necklace, a hairbrush, a snip of silk ribbon, and a department-store sampler of perfume, and stuffed them into a shiny makeup bag. Then she spelled, "G-L-A-M-O-U-R." The spell made the ingredients melt together into a shimmery liquid. She took a whiff of the potion and gasped when she saw herself in the mirror. The spell had gone a little too far — her hair was teased out to the max under a wacky hat. She was wearing an oddly cut glittery gold dress and high heels, and her makeup made her look like an alien.

"Holy cats," B told her reflection. "I look more like a clown than a fashion model." It was not at all what she had in mind.

Next she combined a pink hair twisty, a sparkly lip gloss, a polka-dot sock, and a smiley-face T-shirt. "S-T-Y-L-E," she spelled. Her hair formed itself into two pigtails. Her sweatshirt transformed into a denim jacket, and pink and yellow daisy embroidery appeared all over her jeans. Lace ruffles poked out from under the cuffs of her pants, trimming the edges of her socks.

"Well," B told Nightshade, her black cat, who rubbed against her ankles, "it's a cute look, but maybe a little cutesy for what I was picturing for the competition. I've got to keep trying."

She pawed through her trinkets and experimented with different combinations. Finally she combined a dangly earring, a blusher brush, a Black Cats fan pin, and a black mock railroad-worker's cap. What to spell? Aha. She found the perfect word.

"A-T-T-I-T-U-D-E." She breathed in a smidgeon of the pink potion. And before you could say, "Black Cats," B's clothes transformed once more. She looked like one of Trina's backup dancers, decked out in camouflage cargo pants, a hot-pink T-shirt, and a leather vest, with purple high-top sneakers, and glittery bangles clinking at each wrist.

"Awesome," B whispered. She poured the potion from the makeup bag into a little plastic vial, and slipped it in her purse so she'd remember to put it in her pocket tomorrow. "Potion's done, anyhow," she told herself — and Nightshade, in case he was listening.

Just then Dawn stuck her head through the door. She looked like she was about to say something, but at the sight of B's fashion getup she stopped. "What's all this?"

B felt sheepish. "Oh, I was just working on a potion for tomorrow's Young Witch Competition."

"A makeover potion?" Dawn said. She spied the makeup pouch in B's hands. "A bag-cauldron concoction? My special trademark? That's what you're doing?"

"Well, you made it look so cool, and it was all I could think of," B said, feeling awful.

"What else are you going to steal from me?" Dawn snapped. "First you sneak into the tryouts and try to cheat and use magic to win. Now you steal my recipe for a makeover potion?"

"Not your recipe," B said. "Just the general idea. And Dawn, I wasn't trying to audition . . ."

"I don't want to hear any more about it." She pulled the door shut.

B sighed. She hated having Dawn mad at her. But what could she do if Dawn wouldn't let her explain?

B practiced her storytelling spell until her mom called her down for dinner. B tried hard to keep plot, character, action, theme, setting, and motivation all clearly in mind each time she cast her spell. She'd gotten to the point where her spell could tell a passably decent fairy tale each time, even if somebody usually got eaten by a troll. But, B figured, fairy tales were sometimes like that. Maybe she really did have a shot at winning the competition.

B went downstairs to the kitchen table to find a skillet full of sizzling onions, peppers, and chicken strips, and a plate of steaming tortillas. Fajita night! Her mother's Mexican cooking kick clearly hadn't run its course yet. Everything smelled delicious. Her mom, who never ceased muttering rhyming spells to herself when cooking, spoke some words that made a pan of black beans, and another of Spanish rice, magically transport themselves onto the table. The family sat down to eat.

"This dinner," B's mom said, snatching her magical chopping knife before it could dice the tomatoes too fine, "is an early celebration of Dawn's talent competition tomorrow night and B's Young Witch Competition. You'll both do a wonderful job, I'm sure. We're so proud of you."

B's dad helped himself to a tortilla and loaded it up with fajita fixings. "I just can't believe both competitions happen on the same night," he said. "Of all the rotten luck! Two superstar daughters competing, but I only get to see one."

"Yeah," Dawn said, taking a mouthful of rice. "Who's going to go see which competition?"

Their mother's face fell. "Oh, it's such a shame that we have to choose," she said. "Your father and I finally flipped a coin. Dawn, your father will be there to watch you compete, and B, I'll come to the M.R.S. to watch you."

B dug into her dinner. She felt torn between being sad that her father couldn't come watch her and wondering if she wanted *anyone* there. That storytelling spell . . . Was it reliable enough to demonstrate in public?

"Now, remember, both of you," Mr. Cicely said, "whatever happens tomorrow, your mother and I are so proud of you. So just relax and don't worry about a thing."

"But be sure to do your best," Mrs. Cicely added. "Don't be *too* relaxed."

"I find," Mr. Cicely added, "that when I have a big meeting or presentation at work that I'm worried about, it takes the nervousness away if I just imagine all the people I'll be speaking to wearing polka-dotted underwear."

"Felix!" Mrs. Cicely scolded. "What a thing to say to the girls! Underwear . . ."

"B," her dad said, "remember, if they ask you who developed the first permanent invisibility potion, it's a trick question. It wasn't Wallace Waxby. It was Abigail Waxby. She was his wife, and she was trying to make him invisible because he was so ugly. But he got all the credit because she accidently inhaled some potion and was never seen again."

"The things you say, Felix!"

"Just being helpful, Stella," Dad said. "Excellent dinner, tonight, my dear."

B smiled.

"I don't know why we're all in such a fuss," their mom said. "B, you just focus on your high kicks and, Dawn, you just brush up with your Quickfire Questions flash cards, and we'll all be fine."

"*We'll* be fine?" Dawn said. "*You* need to get your daughters straight, Mom."

They all laughed. Mr. Cicely raised his glass. "To the talented ladies in my home," he said. "To Dawn, the incredible dancer, and to B, the up-and-coming young witch, and to their beautiful mother, whose cooking is the best in the witching world, bar none, even if she was robbed at last year's Witchin' Kitchen Competition by whatshername's butter-scotch crème brulée. Cheers." They clinked their glasses together.

Chapter 12

Friday evening, the butterflies in B's stomach were so fluttery, she had to try three different socks on her left foot before she got the one that matched her right. She considered using a dab of her attitude beauty potion to snazz up her looks, but decided she didn't dare. She'd already sniffed it once. Would sniffing it again use up all its magic? It was possible. And then where would she be?

She reached for a pot of lip gloss stored in the bathroom medicine cabinet. Just then, Dawn barged in, looking for something.

"Good luck tonight, Dawn," B said. Dawn made a grunt of acknowledgment, and B figured that was about the best she would get from her sister tonight. B couldn't wait until their argument blew over.

"Dawn, let's go!" their dad called up the stairs. "I want to get a good parking spot."

"Wish we could just transport there," Dawn grumbled. B was just glad that Dawn had finally spoken to her.

Their mom appeared. "Are *you* ready to transport, B?"

"I guess so," B said. "But could I hold your arm while you do it? I feel so nervous. I sort of want to conserve my magic for the competition."

B's mom smiled. "Of course." She planted a kiss on Dawn's head, then took B's arm, recited a spell, and together they whisked away. They arrived in the coat room at the M.R.S. and hung up their things. B's mom took a seat in the audience while B hurried to find Trina.

"I was wondering where you were," Trina said. "It's almost time to start. Knock 'em dead, B!"

"Same to you," B said. Trina didn't seem anywhere near as nervous as B felt, but that made sense. Trina was used to performing with the Black Cats. As for B, even just reading an assignment in front of her English class was enough to ruin her day.

Before B had much time to think, the Quickfire Questions began. She waited in the wings as the first young witch went on. Someone actually did get the permanent invisibility potion question. B nearly laughed out loud. The contestant, a nervous eleven-year-old boy, answered, "Wallace Waxby," instead of his wife, Abigail. Madame Mel gave him partial credit.

And then it was B's turn. She stepped out onto the stage. This was twenty times worse than a class spelling bee and more terrifying than the audition with Mozart. The great round library room looked different tonight. All the desks and tables had been cleared away, and hundreds of chairs brought in to make room for the magical community, and espe-cially the parents and family members of the young witches present. The stage stood against one side of the room and, below it, the table where Madame Mel sat judging the competition. Lights flooded the stage, making it hard for B to see clearly. The butterflies in her stomach suddenly felt more like woodpeckers.

"Name one of the legendary witches memorialized in the foundation stones of the M.R.S.," Madame Mel said.

B's mind went blank. She had no idea whose name was carved in the foundation stones! A legendary witch? All she could do was guess.

Then she remembered. Back when she'd first gotten her magic, she'd learned about a legendary witch because of a cheap circus performer claiming to be her long-lost umpteenth granddaughter. It was worth a try.

"Morgan Le Fay," she said, surprised at how loud her voice sounded. There must be magical microphones at work.

"That is correct," Madame Mel said. "What is one of the prohibited forms of magic?"

B knew that one well from having violated this rule with George. "Human transformations," she said. "You shouldn't turn people into something they're not." Such as part-mice, she thought ruefully. But at least that had been an accident.

"Very good," Madame Mel said. "Last question. What is the best way to choose a cauldron when making potions?"

Cauldrons. Cauldrons. B tried to think. She'd studied potions with Mr. Bishop in the Magical Rhymatory, but cauldrons were supplied as part of the lab equipment. There was never anything about how to choose them, was there? There had been a textbook, *Pre-teen Potions.* Had there been anything in there about choosing cauldrons?

She was taking too long. She could feel all the eyes of the audience upon her, even though she couldn't see their faces well.

Then she remembered her makeover potion, and how she brewed it up in a cosmetic pouch, much like Dawn had done. A *bag-cauldron*!

That was it!

But when Dawn crossed her mind, she remembered Jason and his tricks. She wondered if her sister was okay.

"Ahem." Madame Mel cleared her throat.

Focus, B!

"A basic cauldron is okay," B said, "but it's even better if the cauldron is a container that fits the . . . mood or the subject of the potion you're trying to brew. Then it, er, lends its qualities to the concoction."

"An excellent answer, B," the Grande Mistress said. "Very perceptive."

The audience broke out in applause. B only barely heard it. She turned and walked off the stage, so happy and relieved she nearly collided with the next contestant. B found Trina and they sat together on a couch in the hallway surrounding the main library room. There were lots of young witches milling around, waiting for their turns.

B looked at her watch. "The talent show semifinals will have begun by now," she said. "I wonder how much longer until the Special Spell part of our competition begins."

Trina gave her a suspicious look. "Why?"

"It's Dawn," B said. "I'm worried about her. Even though she's mad at me right now . . . I know Jason is going to play dirty. Isn't there a break between Quickfire Questions and Special Spells?"

"Yes, there's a short break," Trina said, "but what difference does that make? There's nothing you can do from here, B. Dawn will figure things out on her own."

"I can be quick. Maybe I can help!"

"This is risky, B," Trina said, looking around. "You could miss something and lose your place in the competition."

"Trina," B said, "we know Jason's up to something. We saw him steal . . . whatever that was." Could she get there and back in time? Of course she could. She'd just take a quick look around and be back before anyone noticed anything.

"I won't be gone long," B said. "I promise. Cover for me, okay?"

Before Trina could answer, B spelled, "T-R-A-V-E-L." She vanished in a swirl of magical wind.

B had meant her transportation spell to take her just outside the auditorium at the school, so naturally, she landed in the wings offstage. Better than landing on the stage, at least. A cameraman spotted her. It wasn't Ed.

"Hey," he said. "Where did you come from?"

"Sorry," B said. "I'll just be a second." She peered through the curtains. Jason was about to go on! Jenny Springbranch was there in a special costume, whooping up the crowd while the sinister music filled the auditorium. B ground her teeth as she watched Jason perform his act perfectly. He'd even added a few special touches like having Jenny blindfold him after he had the straitjacket and the handcuffs on. What a show-off!

B tiptoed out of the wings, down the stairs in the outer hallway, and into the back of the auditorium. There, just in front of the stage, was the panel of judges. Clifton Davro was in the middle. A soap opera star wearing a glamorous red dress covered with sparkles, her hair all piled on her head in an elegant 'do, was on his left. On his right was a famous baseball player, wearing a baggy white T-shirt and cap. They were just about to give Jason his score when B spotted her father, just a few rows ahead in the audience. Oh, no! She'd be in big trouble if he saw her here. She took a step backward and nearly toppled a temporary lighting stand.

"I saw Jason Jameson's act in the auditions, earlier this week, and I was impressed then," Clifton Davro was saying, his voice booming over the auditorium's sound system. "But I'm even more impressed now. That young man is a natural showman."

"Yeah, pretty cool," the baseball player said. "But I wish he had cut his assistant in half."

"Oh, stop it, Rocko," the soap star giggled. "Jason was amazing. He doesn't need to change a thing."

Chapter 13

No sign of Dawn, and no sign of trouble from Jason, yet. B backed slowly toward the stage door, watching everything except where she was going. She stumbled into someone carrying a walkie-talkie. It was George!

"What are you doing here?" she whispered.

"I'm helping Ed with the backstage cameras," George said. "They film all the performers going on and off. Pretty much everything that goes on; then they use it later. Isn't that great? I'm Ed's gofer. That means I 'go-for' whatever he needs me to get. Get it? He remembered me from the cafeteria, and asked me after school if I'd like to come tonight and help out. It's really fun."

"Fantastic, George!" B said. "What a lucky break."

"Hey," George said, "aren't you supposed to be at your competition tonight?"

"Yes," B said. "I came back here to see what Jason Jameson was up to. He stole *something*, and I know he's got something nasty up his sleeve. He kept saying there was no way Dawn could beat him. He must be trying to cheat."

George frowned. "With Jason, I think we have to assume he'll try. Come with me. I want to check something out."

Off in the far rear corner of the stage, where old props and boxes were jumbled together, George fished out a backpack. "I saw Jason leave this here earlier," George said. "I figured it had props for his show. But it's still here, and his act is done."

"Open it," B said. "It's got to be a clue."

George peered into the bag. He lifted out a tall clear bottle.

"*Oil?*" they both said together.

"There are four of these in here," George said. "Is this how he got out of his handcuffs? By making them slippery?"

"I don't think he'd need quite this much," B said.

Just then, a producer backstage announced it was time for the next act to go on.

Time.

B looked at her watch. "Holy cats! The Special Spell competition has already started. I've got to get back to the M.R.S.!" She took a deep breath. She'd made it here, but solved nothing. Jason Jameson was still on the loose. "Keep an eye on Jason for me, will you?"

B left through a backstage door and ran down the school corridor until she was far from where anyone could see her. "T-R-A-V-E-L," she said, and her transportation spell whisked her to the M.R.S. She tried to return to the couch where she and Trina last were, but instead she arrived outside the door to the ladies' restroom. She had to sprint halfway around the great circular building to find Trina and the other contestants.

"Where have you been?" Trina whispered. "I was worried that I might have to go find you. Special Spells has started. Someone's out there now doing a spell to make flowers grow. It's taking a while."

B collapsed on the couch, too out of breath to say much.

"You're all red in the face," Trina said. She fanned B off with her competition program. "Did you see anything? Has Jason sabotaged Dawn's act?"

B shook her head. "Not yet," she said. "I saw the end of his act. The judges loved it. Dawn hasn't gone on yet."

From inside the M.R.S. library, they could hear the sound of polite applause. A tall, sad-looking young witch left the stage clutching a pair of nearly empty flowerpots. Uh-oh.

"I'm up next," Trina said, "and you're after me. Wish me luck."

"You'll be great, Trina," B said. "Your spell is amazing."

Trina smiled nervously, then strode onto the stage like the experienced performer that she was. B peeked through the doorway to watch.

Madame Mel gave Trina a nod, and Trina sang her song-casting spell. Her voice reached into every corner and crevice in the great library. B saw people seated on the upper mezzanines crane their necks for a better look. That was the kind of voice she had.

When she'd finished singing, her spell swirled around Madame Mel, teasing loose some strands of her blue hair. A jazzy, big-band-style tune began to play, and a baritone singer sang a song about dancing shoes.

The audience clapped and laughed, especially, B noted, the older ones. Madame Mel's face flushed beet red as the magical music video showed a tall, thin woman with shiny black hair, looking suspiciously like a much younger Madame Mel, dancing at an old-fashioned nightclub with a tall soldier in his dress uniform.

B shook her head and smiled. Trina's spell didn't

just write songs; it wrote love songs that brought back people's most tender memories. Jumping jinxes, that was good magic.

B was so caught up in Trina's spell that she forgot that she was next, until Trina ran off the stage and gave her a friendly high five. "You're up, B!"

B headed out into the bright lights once more. Now was the time for her story spell. Now or never.

Madame Mel dabbed her eyes with a tissue and nodded for B to begin. B licked her lips but they felt as dry as sandpaper. She took a deep breath. She closed her eyes.

She thought about the library—the library where she now stood, and all the libraries she'd ever loved. She thought of the couches, the beanbag chairs, her bed, and all the places she'd ever spent happy hours curled up with a book. She let her mind wander through book after book, like a phantom spirit passing along the shelf, from stories of home and stories of school and stories of lands far away. She felt the places, the characters, the danger, the excitement, the romance, the suspense, the indulgence, the delight.

"S-T-O-R-Y," she said, and as she did so, she knew for the first time just what a glorious, powerful, magical word it was.

A warm, pleasant, crackly voice began to tell a story. It sounded a bit like B's own Granny Grogg. Books slid out from their library shelves and began dancing in midair around the great round library room.

"Once upon a time," the voice said, "in a forest, high in the mountains, a woman lived with her beautiful younger sister, Flora."

B was delighted to see that while the story unfolded, brown books floated down and gathered together to form a mountain behind B. Green books formed trees, and a few red books gathered together to make a little cabin on top of the mountain.

"One spring day, a prince ambled up the path to where Flora and her older sister lived. He spied Flora picking spring flowers, and stopped in his tracks. He fell in love instantly and asked for Flora's hand in marriage, but her older sister refused. 'How can I give away my Flora?' she asked. 'You must pass three tests to prove that you are worthy.' "

The story went on. Even B forgot that she was standing on a stage in front of hundreds of people, the story was so exciting. When it ended, with Flora herself helping the prince complete the final challenge so they could be together, Madame Mel clapped enthusiastically. B was startled to realize that the applause was for her, not just for the story.

"Congratulations," Madame Mel said. "You pass this level."

"That was amazing!" Trina cried, as soon as B rejoined her in the hall. "We're both going on to the final round!"

B squealed along with her friend and jumped up and down — then slipped on something and lost her balance. It was a patch of mud from the flowerpot spell. B sat on the ground, looking at the smeared wet soil. And then it hit her — that was what Jason wanted with so much oil. Slippery, trip-over-and-hurt-yourself oil! She had to warn Dawn.

"How much time did that take?" B asked, switching gears immediately. "Do you think there's been enough time for Jason to sabotage Dawn's act at the talent competition?"

"B . . ." Trina said, shaking her head. "Your mom's headed this way. It looks like she wants to congratulate you."

"Keep her busy for me, please," B begged. "Stall her. I only need a second to warn Dawn about Jason. I just hope I'm not too late!" And before Trina could stop her, B transported back to the school and arrived in the wings. She spotted George right away.

"George!" B gasped. "Where's Jason?"

"I don't know," George said, looking worried. "I think he saw me following him and gave me the slip."

"The slip is right," said B. "He's going to put that oil on the floor to sabotage Dawn — she could really hurt herself if she dances on it!"

George frowned. "We've got to stop him."

The current act was only performing in the area in front of the curtain, so they could cross the stage without being seen. But after two steps, they both fell right onto their backs. Jason had already smeared oil all over the back part of the stage — the part where Dawn did her big running jump.

George picked himself up. "Dawn is next," he said. "We've got to stop her from performing!"

Chapter 14

With effort, B got to her feet and slid back the way they had come, into the wings. They had to find Dawn!

B peeked through a gap in the curtains. A girl was making her trained Jack Russell terrier dance on his hind legs while balancing a dog biscuit on his nose. Beyond the girl and her dog was the judges' table, and in the front row of the audience sat the other contestants. There, closest to B, sat Jason Jameson, grinning broadly as if he was the only one who knew a huge joke. He chewed loudly on a thick wad of gum.

"We'll never find her in time," B worried aloud.

"I'll go get a mop and a bucket," George said, "and I'll . . ."

"There's no time for that," B said. "Even if you could mop it, it'd still be wet. No, George. *You* can't clean this floor. But I can. Stand guard so nobody sees me. C-L-E-A-N!"

B concentrated on the floor, on a safe, sturdy floor that would let Dawn do all her jumping moves flawlessly. Magical bubbles and suds appeared and vanished over the entire surface of the spill. There was a whiff of French fries in the air for just a second, and then the whole mess disappeared, as if it had never been there.

"Wow," George said. "No matter how often you do that, I still can't get used to it."

B barely heard him. "This isn't over yet," she whispered. "Who knows what else he might try? I've got to warn Dawn to be careful, and to keep an eye out for Jason. Where would she be?"

"The acts get to warm up beforehand, and hang out afterward, in the band room," George whispered. "Let's go."

They hurried across the hall to the band room. Kids of all ages were there, dressed in costumes and makeup. At first B couldn't see past a half dozen mimes, but then she saw Dawn, chatting with Jenny Springbranch. What would *she* be doing here? Something connected to Jason, no question. A troupe of acrobatic cheerleaders made a human tower right in front of B, nearly poking a hole in the band room ceiling, and B lost sight of Dawn once more.

"Dawn Cicely," Nancy the director called, poking her head in the door. "One-minute warning!"

B made her way toward Dawn. When her sister saw B, her mouth dropped open in shock. "What are you doing here?" she hissed. "You're supposed to be at the . . . somewhere else!"

"Wait, Dawn, listen," B said. "Jason Jameson is trying to sabotage you!"

Dawn frowned at her, almost like she didn't believe what B said. "I've got to go," she said, and ran out of the room. B just had time to race after her before the music began.

Dawn danced perfectly. Despite everything, B was proud. She couldn't say which she enjoyed more—watching Dawn dance, or watching the angry look on Jason's face when the judges gave her a standing ovation. Dawn took her final bow and rejoined B offstage, out of breath.

A set of triplets went on and did a skit; then Clifton Davro took the microphone. "All you contestants should be proud of yourselves tonight. You've all got tremendous talent to have made it this far. We can't quite decide who to take on to the TV show, so we want to see five acts one last time. They are: Katie Bell, Calum Gardner, Deirdre Fink, Jason Jameson, and Dawn Cicely. Only one act can make it to the national TV show and show us that *You've Got It!*"

Chapter 15

B peeked through the curtains to see how Jason reacted to the announcement. He didn't seem happy at all that he was still a finalist. He gritted his teeth and stormed out the side auditorium door.

He's got something else planned, B said to herself. *I know that look.*

She took off to intercept Jason in the halls, but she didn't get far. A hand grabbed her arm. It was Trina!

"B, come *on*," she said. "I just finished presenting my potion and you're up next!"

B froze. After Jason's cruel tricks, she'd almost forgotten she was supposed to be at the M.R.S.! She thought of how hard she'd worked on her Young Witch Competition. Her potion was in her pocket.

She really wanted to win. But Dawn had been working even harder to win the talent show. If B left now, she knew Jason would try another stunt.

A squeal erupted from backstage. "That's Dawn!" B cried. B, George, and Trina ran — to find a shocked Dawn, standing in the wings, covered in dripping paint! And there stood Jason, only a few steps away.

Trina grabbed a nearby roll of paper towels and started trying to clean Dawn up.

"Geez, Dawn, I'm so sorry," Jason said, with a face that clearly showed otherwise. "It was an accident. I tripped."

B leveled a pointing finger at him. "This was no accident, Jason," she said, "and you know it."

Jason sneered back at her. "Oh, yeah, Hornet Head? Prove it."

"I don't need to prove it," B said. "I know what you did with the oil. This is the last act of sabotage from you tonight. It's going to be a fair fight between you and my sister for the TV spot."

"What oil?" Dawn was clearly annoyed, wiping

down her arms, while Trina cleaned off her legs. "What are you talking about, B?"

"Yeah, Wonder Wasp," Jason sneered. "What oil? You can't prove anything."

George's eyes grew wide. "Oh," he said. "Oh. Boy, oh, boy. You want some proof?" He snapped his fingers and ran off.

"What's going on here?" Dawn demanded. She turned to Jason and glared down at him. "Have you been trying to sabotage me?"

George came running back with Ed, who was rolling a camera. Nancy wasn't far behind. When Nancy saw Dawn covered in paint, she gasped. "Dawn, you've got to get cleaned up!"

While their attention was on Dawn, Jason tried to edge away.

"What's your hurry, Jason?" Trina said.

"Now, everyone," George said. "Let me explain. I've been back here, helping Ed set up cameras and everything else. I know he's rigged up cameras all over backstage to catch some of the silly stuff contestants do before and after they go on. And I bet this camera here" — George pushed aside a curtain to reveal a hidden camera — "will have caught something that wasn't so silly. Ed, can you rewind this to about half an hour ago?"

"Sure, George." Ed rested the rolling camera onto a stack of boxes, still pointing at the group, and fiddled with the buttons on the hidden camera. Then, he angled the camera monitor so everyone could see it.

"What do you see, Nancy?" Ed said. "Looks to me like a kid in a magician's costume, squirting two, no, three . . . no, four bottles of oil all over the stage!"

Now Jason really did look scared. He inched toward the door.

"Stop it right there, Jason," B said. "Now there's proof you were cheating."

"That's right," Ed said. "That's you, isn't it? Yep, that's a good shot of your face. Sabotaging the other acts, eh?"

"Is that so?" Nancy looked at Jason.

"He spilled the paint on Dawn, too," B added.

Nancy nodded. "You, young man, are disqualified. I can't believe you would pull rotten stunts like that. Take your props and leave the building. Security will show you out."

"But . . . !" Jason protested.

"Out with you," Nancy said. "Just wait till I tell Cliff."

Chapter 16

Nancy and Ed left to tell the judges about Jason. The first act began, Katie Bell with the Amazing Dancing Princess. Princess, it seemed, was the Jack Russell terrier.

But Dawn still stood there, backstage, forlorn and covered with paint. "Thanks, you guys," she said. "Now, you go back, B. Go with Trina to do what you need to do." She gave B a significant look, but didn't explain more, because George was still there.

"I will in just a second," B said. "Um, George, would you go grab some more paper towels for Dawn?"

George nodded and ran off, leaving B, Dawn, and Trina alone.

B pulled her vial of shimmering pink makeover potion from her pocket. "Use this, Dawn," she said. "It'll fix up your look in a hurry. I want you to win this competition."

"But, B!" Trina protested. "You *need* your potion. You'll be disqualified!"

"I can't let you do this, B," Dawn said. "I can manage on my own. Go back to the M.R.S."

"My mind's made up," B said, and before Dawn could argue anymore, B uncorked her little bottle and waved it under Dawn's nose. A sweet, perfumey scent filled the air.

Dawn took a deep breath. Her hair lifted as though a wind had blown it. The paint vanished from her clothes as though a big eraser had wiped it away, but the spell didn't stop there. Her clothes transformed completely, until Dawn looked like a professional dancer, all set to perform in a Black Cats video. Her dark jeans became silvery pants with a faux-snakeskin finish. Her shoes turned into shiny black cowboy boots. Her T-shirt was replaced by a black tank top and an off-the-shoulder shirt studded with sequins and rhinestones. Snazzy dark eye makeup appeared where there hadn't been any before. Even Dawn's nails got a new airbrushed design.

"Wow, B," Dawn said, grinning. "I can't believe you gave me that. That's one powerful potion you've made!"

B grinned. "It looks better on you than on me."

But that wasn't quite true. Just breathing the scent of the potion had affected both Trina and B. They each had a cool new hairstyle. B corked her little bottle and put the rest of the potion back in her pocket. Maybe, if she was lucky, it would still have some potency. And maybe, if she was really lucky, she'd still make it to the M.R.S. in time to use it.

Just then Nancy came back to where they stood. "Wow, young lady," she said, observing Dawn. "That was quite the quick costume change!"

Dawn grinned. "Yes, ma'am. I had a little help."

"I should say so. Well, are you ready to go on? You're next after Katie Bell."

Dawn nodded.

"In that case, where's your music?"

Dawn's face fell. "Isn't the CD still in the stereo? I just performed. I haven't touched it since then."

Nancy shook her head. "Nope. I've got all my sound techs looking for it."

"I know what happened," B said. "Jason. His final parting shot. I'll bet he's laughing all the way home."

"Well, what are you going to do?" Nancy said. "Do you have another CD?"

Now any thought of getting back to the M.R.S. was gone.

"Um, sort of," B said, before Dawn could get a word in. "Leave it to us. We'll be ready when it's time for Dawn to go on."

"Huh?" Dawn said. "We will?"

B nodded at Nancy. "We've got another, er, version of the Black Cats album with us," she said, and Nancy walked away.

"What've you got planned, B?" Dawn said. "You seem to be two steps ahead of me everywhere I go."

"And now, for our last act," the announcer's voice said. *"Daaaaaawn Cicely!"*

"Just go!" B cried, giving Dawn a friendly push. "Go dance, and leave the rest to us!"

Dawn headed for the opening curtain, while B and Trina huddled out of sight off in the wings.

"Do you have one more singing spell in you tonight, Trina?" B said. "I need 'Swagger.' Starting now!"

Trina's eyes grew wide; then she nodded, closed her eyes, and softly began to sing the incantation of her songwriting spell. By the time Trina was in position, the music began thumping throughout the auditorium. It was "Swagger" all right, but like no one had ever heard it — a special remixed version that was even more exciting to dance to. And when the magical recording began to sing, Trina joined in, harmonizing along with her own voice.

B pulled out one of her shoelaces and whispered, "M-I-C-R-O-P-H-O-N-E," and her shoelace became a magical mike. Trina belted out a wordless vocal that wandered over and under her own voice singing the main melody line. The crowd went wild, and Dawn picked up on the energy, dancing like never before, adding new twists to the choreography. Every move came off like a charm, right down to the final twirl during Trina's last line.

The crowd leaped to its feet, cheering and screaming for Dawn. B screamed and cheered, too, not caring who heard her. She thought her heart would burst right out of her chest with pride.

The judges stood and joined in Dawn's ovation. Clifton Davro himself climbed up on the stage and put an arm around Dawn's shoulder. "You've got it, Dawn Cicely," he said. "You've got a place on the national television show. *You've got it!*"

Chapter 17

"Okay, B," Trina said. "It's time now. Let's go." And before B could protest, Trina linked arms with her and sang a short transportation spell.

They arrived back at their couch outside the M.R.S. library. Trina, it seemed, had practiced her traveling spells more than B.

B's mom sat there on the couch, clutching her purse and talking in worried tones with Mr. Bishop. At the sight of her daughter, she jumped up. "Where have you been, B?" she cried. "You've been disqualified from the competition, and you've worked so hard. What could possibly—"

"And now," came Madame Mel's magically magnified voice, interrupting what B knew was going to be a super-duper lecture from her mom, "for the announcement of the winners!"

"Come on!" B said. "Let's get inside to hear the results. Then I can explain everything."

Trina, B, her mom, and Mr. Bishop scurried back inside the library. They took their seats just as Madame Mel unfolded the slip of purple parchment and read, "It is with great pleasure that I announce this year's winner. Her singing spell and her dancing potion delighted us all. Please welcome the new Young Witch of the Year, Miss Katrina Lang!"

Trina gasped. B tackled her with a huge hug, then shooed her up and onto the stage.

Even Trina seemed nervous as she stood before the tall and imposing Madame Mel.

"May I see your bracelet, please, young lady?"

Trina held out her wrist with the silver bracelet given to every witch, that held charms representing milestones in their magical education. Trina's carried a single charm from when she found her magic. Madame Mel chanted:

"Each young witch is a gift, full of untapped
  ability,
But talent we honor. It brings responsibility
To hold up your example, to lead and to teach.
This star represents how high you should
  reach."

And there, on Trina's charm bracelet, appeared a glittering silver star.

B felt her eyes grow wet. Trina deserved this award. B didn't begrudge her that charm, not one single bit. She couldn't be prouder of her talented, loyal friend.

"Don't be upset with B, Mrs. Cicely," Trina said afterward, in the lobby. "Jason Jameson tried to sabotage Dawn. B gave up her chance in the Young Witch Competition, and even donated her potion, to help Dawn with her costume after Jason dumped paint all over her."

B's mom's expression changed. She grabbed B and squashed her close in a huge hug. "Did you really do that for your sister, B?" she said. "You were doing so well in the Young Witch Competition. But you gave it all up for Dawn? Oh, honey."

B put her arms around her mother. For a minute, then, B realized just what she had given up. In the moment, she hadn't even questioned what she needed to do for Dawn. Had she really been doing that well in the Young Witch Competition? Could she, maybe, have had a shot at winning? That potion of hers sure did have amazing results.

But it didn't matter. B didn't regret her choice one bit. Seeing Dawn's spectacular last dance was worth everything.

"Good for you, B," Mr. Bishop said. "But Madame Mel's not too happy with you right now. It's never happened before that someone didn't show up when their name was called for the final potions round. I'll go smooth things over with her." He smiled. "If there's one thing she hates, it's foul play. She'll be proud of you for thwarting Jason. And, incidentally, I'll make sure the school principal hears about Jason's antics tomorrow."

* * *

After the hubbub at the M.R.S. had died down, B's mom invited everyone back to their home for an impromptu party. "Butterscotch ripple cheesecake with homemade peach custard at our house!" she cried, and nobody needed a second invitation. Trina and her grandmother came, along with Mr. Bishop, and when they got there they found Dawn and Mr. Cicely waiting for them. Dawn wore a silk banner draped over her shoulder, announcing "You've Got It!" in gold letters.

After their mom had hugged Dawn about twenty times, she started serving up dessert, and Dawn sat down at the kitchen table next to B. Trina had insisted on telling everyone what B had done, and how much she'd sacrificed to help Dawn.

Dawn's eyes were wide. "So you missed the potions round?"

B nodded. "It's okay. It was worth it to see you dance so well. I am really proud of my superstar sister."

Dawn threw her arms around B. "*You're* the superstar," Dawn said, starting to sound a little weepy. "I'm sorry I was so mad at you this week," she whispered in B's ear.

B hugged her back. "That's okay."

Their mom set plates of incredible dessert in front of both of them, but Dawn paid no attention to hers. "You may not have won the Young Witch Competition, but you're the star in my book," she said. "Here. I want you to have this. You deserve it."

Dawn reached for her silver bracelet and removed her own star charm. She handed it to B.

B took the charm and stared at it. Only then did she realize that everyone else in the room was watching them. They burst into applause!

B hugged her sister again. "Thanks, Dawn."

"Thank *you*," Dawn said. "When it comes to being a great sister, *You've Got It!*"

Don't miss any of the M·A·G·I·C!
B Magical #1: The Missing Magic

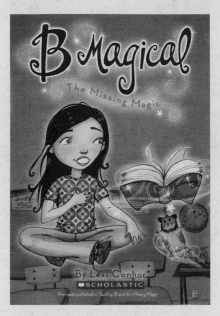

Now that Beatrix (known to her friends as B) is eleven, she should be able to cast spells, just like everyone else in her magical family. But no matter how hard she tries, B is still an ordinary girl.

Then one day at school, everything changes. B discovers that there's more than one kind of spelling — and that the F-U-N is just beginning!

Beatrix (B for short) loves her new magic lessons. But when the circus comes to town, along with a "witch" named Enchantress Le Fay, B is put to the test. B is sure Le Fay isn't a real witch, but when she puts a hex on B's best friend, George, bad things really happen.

B needs to act fast — before George and the whole witching community get into real T-R-O-U-B-L-E!

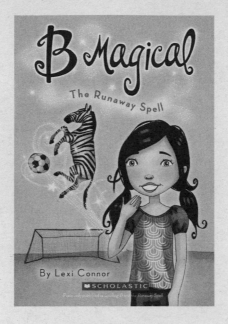

Now that B's best friend, George, knows that she's a witch, he wants to see what she can do. And with the big championship soccer game coming up, George asks for B's magical help — can she make him play like his favorite soccer star, the Italian Zebra?

But B's spell takes a wild turn, and soon George is more zebra than boy! Can she make his tails and ears V-A-N-I-S-H before the big game?

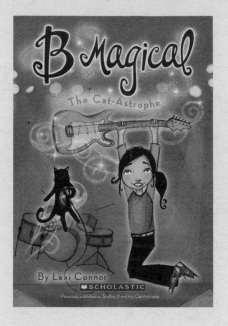

Beatrix and her best friend, George, are excited when a new girl joins their class at school. Trina seems nice, but she also seems to have a lot of secrets. When strange things start happening whenever B and George are around Trina, B can't help but wonder—could the new girl be a witch, too? And maybe even . . . a secret pop S-T-A-R?

Beatrix loves that her dad works at Enchanted Chocolates — after all, who wouldn't like free candy and special tours of a chocolate factory?

But something goes terribly wrong with the new batch of chocolate-covered fruit. All the witches who try the candy lose their ability to enchant! Can B whip up a solution, or could this spell the E-N-D of the magic?

POISON APPLE BOOKS

The Dead End

This Totally Bites!

Miss Fortune

Now You See Me...

THRILLING. BONE-CHILLING.
THESE BOOKS HAVE BITE!